Potpourri

Potpourri

by Anusha VR

Chapeltown Books

British Library Cataloguing in Publication Data

A Record of this Publication is available from the British Library

ISBN 978-1-910542-21-7

This edition published 2018 by Chapeltown Books
Manchester, England

Contents

Acknowledgements

I owe a debt of gratitude to my aunt, CY Bharathi for putting up with all my shenanigans and for helping me find humour even in the darkest of times. I'd be lost in this crazy world without her. A shoutout to my parents – Chotu and CV; plus Amigo for always having my back.

And to my editor, Gill James, for being the epitome of patience when I made last minute changes to the manuscript. This book would've never seen the light of day if she hadn't taken a chance on me.

Introduction

Somewhere between working twelve hour shifts at a tax firm and cramming for exams, these stories and poems tumbled onto torn sheets and paper napkins. Being a corporate sellout who juggles tax returns all day, I could feel the literary world slipping away from me. *Potpourri* is an attempt at regaining a sliver of that bookish world.

Mrs Maurier's Garden

I curled up by the window in my room with a book in hand. Gossamer like snow fell softly from the sky. My window overlooked Mrs Maurier's garden. Even the biting cold weather hadn't deterred the frail old woman from gardening. It was her garden alone that held a profusion of colours within its brick walls and created a splendid contrast against the sparkling white snow.

Flowering quince threatened to spill its red blossoms over the garden walls, orange witch-hazels glowed like miniature suns while the white Christmas roses blended merrily into the background with only their emerald green leaves visible from a distance. That much needed burst of colour distracted me from the book I was currently reading. My train of thought circled around Mrs Maurier.

She was a quiet old woman. She wasn't the kind to indulge in gossip or show up at Christmas parties. She kept to herself. Mother said the other neighbours initially held a ton of interest in unearthing the eccentricities of Mrs Maurier's life. But all anyone knew was she had moved into the sprawling bungalow after her husband's death. As the years passed by people began to lose interest as they realized she was just a plain old widow who lacked any form of social skill. The only thing remarkable about her was the garden which held a myriad of flora, all year round.

I sympathized with the old lady. I had always been the peculiar kid on the block who'd rather stay home and read a good book than graze your knees playing a pointless and physically strenuous game. I knew what it was like to be judged when your only crime was being an introvert.

Mother always nagged. A constant complaint as to how I never went outdoors like the other kids. I'd sigh and wave her away with my perpetual excuse about not having many kids living in the neighbourhood to play with. Besides quite a few of them had gone missing. Is that what she wanted, I'd ask in a nonchalant tone to get her off my back. She'd reprimand me and walk away.

Someone tapped my shoulder, startling me from my random musings. It was mother.

"Mrs Maurier, has passed away. It happened last night. Her executor is downstairs right now. He said he would like to talk to you."

I was taken aback. A few seconds ago I was awe struck by the old woman's green thumb and now she was dead. I had never really interacted with her despite having her as my neighbour all my life. Apart from the courteous nod she occasionally graced me with, there wasn't a single instance I could recall when I'd actually had a conversation with her. I couldn't fathom why her executor wanted to speak to me.

Why?" I asked in a perplexed tone.

"I'm just as curious as you, kid."

We made our way downstairs. A grim looking man wearing a perfectly pressed navy blue suit stood in the living room.

"I am Mr. Johnson, Mrs Maurier's executor. And you must be Anna," he said in a baritone voice.

I nodded, unable to comprehend why this man was standing in our house.

"Mrs Maurier would like you to have her entire collection of books. Calling it a collection would be an understatement. It's more in the ranks of a library. She said and I quote 'Anna is the only child who never ran amok in the streets whiling away her time pointlessly. She has her nose buried in a book rather than other people's business' I assume the two of you must have been quite close as she held the books very dear to her."

I was touched. Fifteen years she had been my neighbour. Or rather I had been her neighbour. She had practically watched me grow up. Not a word exchanged between us and she had left her enormous book collection to me – a complete stranger.

My mother and I thanked him. He said he would arrange to have all the books delivered to our house once he carried out the remaining aspects of her will.

Years later, when I came home from college during the winter break my mother was bursting with her trademark form of enthusiasm when she stumbled upon some gossip

"Remember Mrs. Maurier?" she asked.

"Ma, just tell me what you have to. I doubt I'd ever forget her considering the hundreds of books sitting in my room for years now. She is the reason I am not splurging all my money on books and…"

"Yea yea. Books *schmooks*. Listen up!" she said cutting me off midway. I gestured for her to continue.

"Well, the new owners are tearing Mrs Maurier's bungalow down since they want to build something more modern in its place. And apparently they found small skulls and bones buried all over her garden. All those children that went missing every few months ended up in her garden. Can you believe that?!"

My mother's morbid fascination disturbed me. I was convinced my mother was conjuring up a juicy piece of gossip just to tease me. I ran up to my room to get a look at the garden. That is when I saw it. The garden was in shambles. Black and yellow tape surrounded the house. The garden had been dug up in multiple spots. That lively place was devoid of anything but dry brown grass and vicious weeds.

A few weeks later, the newspapers confirmed albeit with a more sombre and appropriate tone what my mother had narrated.

Mrs Maurier had killed each one of those children who had gone missing and buried them in that lush green enclosure. Every media outlet was obsessed with this case but what no one could quote figure out was the motive.

Why would a simple widow kill all those innocuous children?

Mrs Maurier's motive was clear to me. She really hated children. I had known each one of the missing kids. And all of them had been whirlwinds of trouble. Shattering her windows with their silly games of catch, sneaking into her garden to steal peaches and uproot flower beds just for the fun of it, mock her as she hobbled along on her way to the grocery store. One would probably say that's just kids being kids. But not all kids wreaked havoc. At least I hadn't been like one of them.

I had been spared the fate she had dealt to them. Perhaps, she saw that I was more like her. The quiet one. The good one.

An Orange Revolution

"Sir, we have lost another one of our comrades." said the Lieutenant in a voice laced with melancholy.

"Who?" asked the Captain through gritted teeth. A low snarl began to form in his throat.

"Vrish at the Delhi Zoo. A human jumped into the enclosure. So they…" Lieutenant Veer's voice trailed off.

This was the third such incident in one year. At one end the animal activists cried themselves hoarse petitioning for "Save Tiger" campaigns while on the other end tigers were shot because humans jumped into their enclosures. This was gruesome fact they all knew too well.

"Perhaps when a burglar enters their house, the cops will shoot the residents of the house to save the burglar" said the majestic Shah pacing back and forth on the mossy forest floor.

A soft giggle escaped from the gathering of younger tigers at the edge of the circle. A glance from Shah in their direction and the silence of the forest was restored and nothing more than the rustling of leaves and the babbling of a brook filed the air.

"It was not even his home. They kept him captive. And then they have the audacity to claim his life all because a human cannot adhere to the rules. What is the use of razing our foliage covered homes to the ground with the excuse of expanding their *civilized* society if they cannot read a sign board at a zoo!" he roared.

Even Lieutenant Veer, who was well accustomed to Shah's moods was taken aback at his unbridled display of anger.

"We will hit back, Sir."

"When?"

"We have our plans…."

"We have been planning for decades, comrade. Decades! And have we achieved anything? We need a revolution!"

"Sir, we…"

"We have stood by and watched atrocities being committed against us like silent spectators. We are royalty. It is about time we were treated like it."

"The humans. All of them are not evil. Some of them fight for us. They have organizations of their own to protect us."

"Protect us? Like how they protected the black buck from that mad actor who went on a shooting spree to flaunt his shooting skills before his co-star? The black buck was murdered fifteen years ago. This farce humans like to call their 'judicial system' is letting that man roam free even today. That case will run in the courts long after your children have been interred in the ground. Maybe the black bucks are alright with idea of being spineless creatures. But when the Royal Bengal Tiger roars the world will listen."

"But they outnumber us, Sir! The humans are in billions. We are merely thousands. It is not pragmatic. It would be a suicide mission." A hint of anxiety became evident in his tone.

Shah's voice did not waver even for a minute.

"You are smart cat, Veer. But you have your numbers jumbled this time around." he said softly, a menacing sparkle in his eye.

"I do not follow, Sir?" Veer said with a quizzical expression.

"Do you honestly believe that it is merely our clan that despises humans? Show me an animal and I will show you a weapon we can use against those imbeciles. They have butchered countless elephants for their ivory, the crocs for their skins and the rhinos for their horns. And these are just a few of the countless horrifying deeds."

"Lobbying all the animals will eat away our time."

"That is the only way we will have numbers and strength on our side."

"Even those who have switched sides?"

A low roar threatened to burst out of Shah. He hated those animals that had betrayed their blood. The dogs. The cats. Those who had turned traitors to side with the humans in order to lead a life of luxury.

"Especially them. It has to start with those rotten traitors. The humans will not know what hit them when their own adorable *pets* turn against them."

"I can send the messenger birds to lobby the cats. But I won't keep my hopes up about the mongrels" said Veer with sheer disdain in his voice. If there was anything he hated more than humans it was the mutts that kept them company.

"Oh they will turn too. Loyalty is a concept for story books to glamorize. Those flea ridden fur balls are not the least bit loyal. They act on a deep rooted instinct of survival just like any other living creature. Offer them food and they will follow you to the ends of the jungle. They will rip their human friends to shreds if we offer them something even the humans cannot. The thrill of the hunt."

The idea began to twist and turn and solidify in Veer's mind. Shah was right. They could pull this off if the other animals backed them up. It was a thing of sheer brilliance. The goal was tough but very much attainable.

"I will set the whole thing in motion, Sir. You do not have to trouble yourself with the menial tasks of approaching the lowly animals."

"I knew I could always count on you, Veer. You must start with the elephants. The forest dwellers may respect us out of fear but they respect the elephants for their wisdom. If we have the elephants on our side it is as good as having half the forest on our side."

"Yes, Sir."

The young Lieutenant's gold speckled orange fur glistened as the sun rays pierced through the forest canopy only to fall on his striped fur. He raced across the jungle towards the closest water body where Shah had said the elephants would be lounging.

Weeks later Shah sat near the banks of the muddy pond. The very same pond where Veer had been captured by poachers who had waited in the emerald thicket.

Shah had been the leader of his clan for nearly a decade now. But along with the passage of time he heard the soft whispers. Thoughts of replacing him ran through every tiger's head but no one had mustered up the courage to declare it. Not yet at least. He knew it was only a matter of time before they unanimously appointed Veer to take his place. The mere thought of it made his fur stand on edge.

Shah had seen a few poorly laid out traps scattered across the forest off late. He knew quite well that the humans would always be on the lookout for a majestic tiger. Some rich business tycoon would undoubtedly want a tiger skin rug to adorn his study. Shah was getting old but he was still sharp as a tack. He made his decision without sparing a second thought. Veer would be a perfect candidate.

Veer had been right about one thing, thought Shah as a smug look spread across his royal visage. It was a suicide mission.

Perhaps greed was the one thing that was the common denominator in all living beings.

Rainbow in the Abyss

She kept her hair hidden like every other inch of her body in layers of black cloth

It was like a terrifying abyss swallowing her whole.

"It is not holy for a woman to entice a man. You must wear it at all times," they said.

Blind obedience from childhood soon transformed into quiet rebellion.

Sparkling blue akin to fairy dust, sunshine yellow, dragon-fruit pink, clover green and purple galaxies streaked her thick mane. In the midst of the black abyss, she harboured her rainbow tresses which she one day hoped to spill out of her *hijab*.

Bibliophile

The rain came pouring down with a vengeance. The tar roads had transformed into slithering masses of black water. The orange hued light spilling from street lamps gave a hazy appearance to the nearby objects. Riding back home in this atrocious weather would be pure madness. Nikhil parked his motorcycle near the pavement and rushed into the nearest ramshackle building.

Bangalore had quite a few of these dilapidated buildings even though it was a bustling metropolitan city. But this one in particular was an old library built back in the day when the British rule prevailed in India.

Nikhil didn't have a penchant for history or libraries. Rather, he fostered a deep aversion to books of any kind. Library or not, it served his purpose of not getting soaked to the bone.

He wondered when the rain would finally relent as he leaned against the door of the library with the porch sheltering him from the vicious downpour. The door caved inwards and threw him slightly off balance.

That's odd, he thought as he straightened himself. He figured it would be much warmer inside and made his way in.

The room was bathed in a warm glow from the lamps on each table. The walls were lined with shelves holding a myriad of books from ceiling to floor. The room appeared to stretch on into infinity. More tables. More books. More shelves.

He looked around and found no one. Sitting down by the table nearest to the door, he pulled out a pack of smokes and lit one.

"Hi there," came a soft voice from somewhere among the shelves.

He was taken aback by the sudden greeting but when he located the source of the voice he smiled.

A young woman clad in a black full length skirt and beige blouse was walking towards him.

"Frightful weather."

"Very."

"You are here to borrow a book, I suppose?" she asked, giving a quizzical stare at his cigarette.

"Yes," he mumbled. He wanted to get rid of the cigarette. He dropped it and crushed it beneath the sole of his shoe the minute she looked away to glance at the shelves.

She wasn't a beautiful woman. She had thick-framed glasses and her hair was tied up in a ponytail. Her face was devoid of any trace of make-up. Yet, she looked pretty in her own minimalistic way. There was no way he was going to look like a insolent fool before her.

"Yes, I wanted to borrow a book. But I'm afraid I'm not carrying my membership card with me tonight." He was proud of making up an excuse so quickly.

"That's alright. You can borrow one nonetheless. After all, libraries run on a system of trust. Trust that you will return the book. Trust that you will come back," she said leading him between the rows of shelves.

He gave her a brief nod and followed her.

Smart girls were always trouble, he thought to himself.

"Go ahead. Pick any book you like," she said waving her arm in the general direction of the books.

He picked up a random book off the shelf, hoping she wouldn't ask him to delve into any details. It had probably been years since he had picked up any book. He wanted to keep up this charade of being a man interested in something as loathsome as books.

"There is a comfort amidst the pages of books, don't you agree? It smells like petrichor and dried flowers mixed together. At least, that is how I would describe it. Oh, I would bottle it up as a perfume if I could! It's downright dizzying! It gives you the feeling of coming home and going away on an adventure at the same time." She said with a slightly dreamy look in her eyes.

He felt bewitched by the way she spoke. He had to admit none of it made any sense to him. Hell, what did petrichor even mean? But he was taken in by all that she had said. He was blindly ruffling through the pages whilst looking at her.

"God dammit!" he cursed. The tip of his index finger had been slit by one of the pages. Two drops of blood had tainted the page. The droplets of blood had the same effect on the book as it would have had if dropped in a jar of water. It began to spread all over the page, tinging the page from dark red in the centre to a tender faded red at the edges.

The library seemed to change oh-so slightly. As though the books had breathed a collective sigh of relief. A light fluttering of pages could be heard despite there being no window left open.

"Joe was right. Nothing is stronger than blood magic. You are bound to this library now."

"Who is Joe? Wait, what are you talking about?"

He tried to place the book back on the shelf but inexplicably he was unable to. It was somehow glued to his hands.

"Joe is the traveling hippie who pops by once in a while. Trying to read up on marijuana laws in the country. Poor thing has been trying to get it legalized for years. Died in a horrifying stampede at one of the rallies he had organized. Such a shame. You'll get to meet him sometime." she said coolly as though she had uttered something mundane.

He tried to step backward. He wanted to put as much distance as he possibly could between himself and this crazed woman. She was clearly delusional. But he stood there, rooted to that spot.

"I was the librarian here. Such a beautiful place this used to be. Not a speck of dust anywhere. All the books in order. I used to go through books as quickly as a painkiller addict pops pills. I had a never ending to-read list. I never did get to finish my list. One night, a fire destroyed the left wing of the library. I was taking stock of the magical realism books that night." Her voice was laced with melancholy. Her sadness seemed to be directed at the loss of books she was taking stock of rather than the loss of her own life.

"It has been awful here. All these books around me and I can't even touch them. See!" she shrieked. Her hand went right through the books grasping at nothing but air.

"If this isn't hell, I don't know what is! But now I have you. You will read for me."

"But why me?" His voice was trembling now.

"Uncultured swines like you who think reading is a thing of the past! Glued to computers and smartphones all day. Bullying the kids who make a trip to the school library instead of whiling away time on a basketball court. Vandalizing books by tearing pages, scribbling notes in the corners, dog-earring the pages, ruining the spine of magnificent books. Smoking a cigarette in a sanctum such as this! Are you trying to burn it to the ground? Think of this as a penance of sorts. And once your heart stops beating, which it eventually will because you humans are such a herculean inconvenience, I will find myself another human who will read for me. And then another."

Stupid people can be held guilty for numerous things. But at the top of the list is not knowing when to stop talking. Even when the ghost of a librarian is going to keep you prisoner for the rest of your mortal life.

"But why can't you just stop reading?" he asked assuming it to be an innocuous question.

"Darling, we are not called bibliophiles for nothing."

The books sighed again. Happy. The reader had found her enabler at last.

Dead Dreams

She had always loved the view from the table placed near the floor length window in the seventh floor cafeteria. It gave her a complete birds-eye view of the grassy sea dotted with trees and flower beds sprawling out beneath her. She had pushed away the tray of food to one side of the table. All her concentration was invested in the notebook placed before her.

She worked furiously at capturing the intricate foliage of the trees and the shadows it casted on the pavement, the sunlight hitting the leaves at just the right angles that made them shimmer like emeralds, the gardener who sat underneath one of the trees feasting on a sandwich after a long warm afternoon of pruning hedges. She wanted to transport that entire view onto paper.

When she reclined to get a look at her work, the forest green smudges on her finger tips distracted her. She was reaching to get a tissue from her handbag when she caught sight of her barely discernible reflection in the window.

Her reflection wrenched her back to reality. It showed her what she actually was. What she would always be.

A woman wearing a sensible pantsuit worrying about the fast approaching deadline for the tax audit

She had a meeting that afternoon, final reviews to be done and reports to be signed. She lived in a grey world devoid of colours.

An A-grade student at school. Graduated with honours at her college.

Youngest partner in one of the biggest accounting firms in the world.

"You must be downright stupid to throw all that away to dabble in paints and scribble on paper. Money trumps passion. The joy of doing what you love won't fill an empty belly, child," her mother had told her years ago.

She didn't foster a dislike towards her mother. She was an immigrant who had raised her daughter all alone in a big city. Tough love was all her mother knew.

An artist had died the day she became an accountant.

The career she had chosen paid the bills.

The career she had chosen didn't disappoint her family. They were proud.

The career she had chosen didn't make the society question if she was successful. They knew she was.

The career she had chosen had wiped away her dreams. As if they never existed.

Every morning she would stand before the mirror and promise herself that this was temporary. She would give it all up and chase her dreams like she was the main lead in a corny movie.

But she never did. The mantras slowly dwindled away along with her courage to follow her heart.

She smiled a sad smile as she slipped the notebook back in her hand-bag and made her way to the meeting.

A Perfect Family

They found her sitting in a pool of blood in the living room. Her dead parents lay in contorted positions. An endless stream of tears flowed down her face. She had cried herself hoarse. It was her loud cries that they heard on their trek back from the nearby waterfall that made them peep into the cabin. Without a second thought, Natalie had rushed into the house and picked up the child. Rick kept trying to reach the police but his cell phone repeatedly displayed the "*NO NETWORK*" message.

Natalie held the bloodied child and checked if she had been wounded. No wounds. The child had stopped crying as Natalie rocked her to and fro.

Richard forgot about the phone call. Natalie forgot about driving back home. They sat on the couch cajoling the six year old and wiping her tears away. They couldn't leave her. Not after what she has been through. What if the vile monster who had hacked her parents came back for her? They couldn't possibly leave this precious thing all alone with her murdered parents. They forgot about the rotting bodies in the living room. Natalie went to find clean clothes with the child tottering behind her and Rick rummaged through the kitchen for some water. The poor darling must be dehydrated by now due to the constant crying.

When they had got her all cleaned up and fed, she smiled. A content smile. She had found her new parents. The child clung to Natalie as the latter stroked her hair. Rick felt a sense of hypnotic happiness lull his senses. This was their home now. They were a perfect family.

Months ago, the parents who now lay dead had found the blue-eyed girl sitting in a pool of blood of her previous parents.

Déjà Vu

The crisp air whipped the faces of the passers-by on the 9th arrondissement of Paris. Everyone was in a hurry to go somewhere. Even the tourists seemed to be making haste. One would think considering the purpose of a tour they might take a moment to look around and soak it all in. Their tour guide who seemed to be the shepherd coaxed the group into Fragonard Musée du Parfum.

A wave of sweet intoxicating fragrances encapsulated them once they set foot inside the perfume museum. After being ensconced in 19th century interiors for the better part of an hour they were led to a quaint looking shop. Right from delicate perfumes to scented candles, various little knick-knacks called out to the tourists to come forth and make their wallets a bit lighter.

Not once did a flicker of second thought appear in their minds as they shelled out exorbitant sums for tiny bottles of sweet-smelling scents. The thought of taking it back home as a sign of visiting the famous perfume museum, nonchalantly suggesting to their friends back at home as to how luxurious these perfumes were and even going to the extent of gifting it to a handful of people to give an aura of being someone who can afford to dole out such lavish gifts, played in almost everyone's mind.

They stepped out gripping their decorative paper bags containing their haul from the museum and made their way to the shuttle.

Always in a hurry. Not even sparing a look towards an old woman seated on the pavement in a corner opposite the museum, the group jostled their way through the crowd.

She had the look of a sun dried peach. She sat there wearing clothes which had seen better days. A shock of grey hair was her crown. But yet, her eyes sparkled like the ocean, hinting at the colourful past she had lived before degenerating into the state she was in today. There was a slight movement at the corner of her coat. For a minute it appeared as though the apparel had a life of its own but on closer inspection it was clear that it was only a kitten which had blended in with the grey washed out clothes draped over the woman.

It purred and clawed and yawned. But the old woman looked at it as if it were the only kitten able to do so.

A few yards away a daughter bickered with her parents about not having bought enough vials of perfume. Snatches of the conversation floated towards the old woman but her thoughts went back to the silver kitten mewling at her side. Her provision of food was running precariously low. She had to scavenge something to keep the little one's heart beating.

The bickering had now escalated to a full-fledged fight. The daughter who was throwing a tantrum was now refusing to eat her lunch which was now being handed out in small boxes to the entire group, before they boarded the bus.

A few months ago the old woman had stumbled upon this ball of fur. Silent and curled up next to the mother who was fogging the pavement with her last breath. And ever since, that silver feline had become her responsibility.

The angry daughter was storming away from her parents and towards the old woman. She threw the box towards the trashcan and running out of ways to express her annoyance she gave a pause and marched back into the bus without acknowledging the pained look on her parents faces.

The box bounced off the rim of the trashcan and landed on the pavement. An inexplicably good shot of luck. She hobbled towards the box and brought it back to her corner. A croissant, an apple and a tiny plastic bottle of orange juice. The worrisome look on her face dissipated. Today would be a good day.

Months later, the silver streak that kept the old woman company had moved on. Moved on like the boys she had raised as a nanny at the Loys Chateau. The kitten was now a cat.

Déjà vu was the only card fate dealt her.

The Carousel

His happiest childhood memory was of him going with his father to the fair that was set up in his neighbourhood every fall. It made him smile when he remembered going on all those rides and eating cotton candy till his tummy hurt. But that was long time ago. Almost felt like another lifetime.

Today, he sat on the bench near the carousel in his own amusement park. The glassy eyed beasts seemed to stare back at him. A tourist had died in a roller coaster ride. A minor flaw in the safety catch. One freak incident was enough to drive away the visitors like the plague had taken hold of the park.

All Gerard had wanted was to recreate a happy figment of his childhood. A simpler time. A happier time. A time when suicide was just an incident the newspaper reported. Not something his father would fall victim to. Ever since the park had gone belly up, his wife had constantly worried about him. She knew her husband was a strong man. But so was his father.

"I just want to say goodbye, Donna. I spent the better part of my life building that place. I think I have earned the right to say goodbye."

He felt a tad foolish for snapping at her. He knew she was only looking out for him. His father's death had always cast its shadow on every aspect of his life. His marriage was no exception.

The park had swallowed up all the funds he had managed to procure. Most of his friends had urged him to get out while he still could. But he had stood his ground. He stood by his dream till the last crumbling moment. Now he was drowning in a pool of debt. But he knew he would survive. He was a fighter. He would find a way out and set things right again.

He got up to walk throughout the deserted park one last time. The carousel creaked and moved. It was the slightest of movements but in that eerie silence, the creak boomed across the park. He spun around to find a little girl standing by the carousel.

"You are not supposed to be here, child. It's closed," he said looking around to see if he could find her parents.

"You are not supposed to be here either," she said in a soft voice.

"I run this place." he sighed.

"Well, you are not doing a very good job," she said as she walked towards him.

He was still looking around for someone to take this bothersome child away when she tugged at his sleeve.

When he looked down at her, he saw that half her skull was crushed in, blood matted her ebony hair, her limbs were covered with numerous cuts and scrapes and her right hand was twisted at an angle that felt painful just to look at.

He took a step back and leaned on the maypole. A knot in his throat barred him from uttering a word. The dusty strips of cloth unwound themselves from the maypole on their own accord and coiled around his neck.

"Recreating your childhood is all fun and games. As long as you don't wreck someone else's," she said as the wide strips of ribbon tightened their grasp around his neck.

"Who..." he sputtered mid-sentence as his lungs felt like they were ablaze.

"The girl who died because cheapness trumps safety. What goes around comes around, just like your beloved carousel."

The jigsaw pieces began to fall in place. He wanted to apologize. He wanted to beg for mercy. He wanted to live. He dangled a few feet above the ground.

"Oops," she muttered as she looked into his lifeless eyes one last time before she walked away. A contented sigh escaped her lips.

Moonlight

Kalyani sat by the river. The air was thick with the scent of gooseberries. She held some berries in the palm of her hand. In an absent-minded haze she popped a few in her mouth. The rest were nibbled away by Chand, the fluffy white rabbit.

"I don't want to leave. This village is my home. This is all I've known," she said, holding back tears.

"You have to take a leap of faith," Chand said and muzzled his pink nose against her elbow.

"Easy for you to say. You're not the one leaving."

Kalyani was being sent to another village to continue her schooling. The mere thought of being surrounded by unknown faces, away from her family, away from Chand, terrified her.

She had perfected a routine for herself in her village – Chillakuru.

The oldest woman in the village who had an affable tooth-less smile and skin like a wrinkled peach conducted lessons under the gigantic peepal tree in the middle of the village. The lessons didn't last for more than two hours. After which Kalyani was left to her own devices.

With Chand in tow she would scour the woods for the brightest flowers and juiciest berries. Swimming in the river, while Chand lazily gnawed the tender grass on the banks was a favourite pastime. More often than not she would come home with bruised knees and bloodied elbows. She liked her routine.

She was a brave girl who never backed away from a challenge. She could climb the highest tree in the mango fields without flinching. But adapting to change frightened her. She didn't want to leave home.

"You have to take a leap of faith," Chand said again, wiggling his fluffy stub of a tail.

"Oh, stop it."

She stomped off towards her house. Chand didn't follow her like he always did. Such futile advice from her most trusted comrade. She was crestfallen.

That night, her mother ushered her to bed early as they had to embark on a long journey the next morning to drop Kalyani off at her new school, her new home. She searched for Chand everywhere but in vain.

Every night he would curl up beside her and doze away. She wondered if she had hurt his feeling earlier. She pushed the thought away and continued to look for him frantically around the house and in the backyard.

Moonlight had thrown her blanket on the village and everything sparkled like silver. Kalyani looked up at the moon which was suspended in a pitch black sky and saw the faintest outline of a rabbit.

She heard Chand's voice:

"When you feel unsure and lost, look up at the sky and I'll be there looking down at you. Remember to muster up all your courage and take a leap of faith."

A sceptic would have said it was merely the breeze rustling the neem leaves.

But Kalyani believed that the universe had a touch of magic. And her comrade words had renewed her strength and subdued her fears.

She looked up at the moon and smiled.

Reverse Metamorphosis

Mrs. Lian was too busy to die.

Edwin would be waiting. Soccer practice must have wrapped up ages ago. She chided herself for not leaving the house an hour early. But the radiator had been giving trouble and she had to hover around the house to ensure the handy man fixed it. And Roller would not eat unless she sat with him, making ridiculous baby voices coaxing him to eat his food and bribing him with a long walk in the park later that evening. Terence had organized a dinner for all the partners at the firm tonight. She had to stop by the dry cleaner's to collect her outfit. She had spent the whole week agonizing over what outfit to wear. Terence loathed the few extra pounds she had put on in the course of their seventeen year marriage. She took the utmost care to hide the extra weight as shedding it was out of the question. She could not give up her comfort food. Not even for Terence.

Pain shot through every inch of her body. She blocked it out as best as she could. But she was unable to grasp her previous train of thought. She seemed to be slipping from the present into the past. Images flashed in her mind like a poorly put together slide show.

She had graduated from law school. She had wanted to set up her own practice. She had wanted to travel the world. She had wanted to dip her toes in the bioluminescent bays of Viques and watch the water light up as though a million stars had exploded right underneath the surface. She had wanted to watch the orange-hued sky lanterns float across the inky black sky during the Yi Peng festival. She had wanted to write a book. She had wanted…

But somewhere along the way she had become Mrs. Lian. Wants did not matter in a world where she was Mrs Lian. At least *her* wants didn't.

It was akin to reverse metamorphosis, if you could term it as such. The butterfly had gone back into the pupa, only for a caterpillar to emerge.

She could see blurred figures clad in shades of grey, blue and white going in and out of her line of sight. A sharp smell of disinfectant had enveloped her surroundings.

But her mind refused to register what was happening. It kept going back. Back to when she was more than just Mrs. Lian. It was like trying to grasp sand. The harder she tried to focus on the current situation, the more she found herself slipping into a melancholic haze of the past.

The back-packing trip across Europe that she never took. The tattoo she never got. The crazy colour she never dyed her hair. The man with the lush accent she never went on a date with. That scuba diving trip with her friends she had never agreed to.

All those years of checking off to-do lists, she had forgotten she had had one of her own years ago. She wanted to scream. It was worse than the physical pain coursing through her body.

She had to survive this. She had to survive this for Edwin. For Terence.

But mostly for herself.

The last thought felt wrong. But was it?

The past began to slip away as swiftly as it had come to her. She was able to piece together what had happened.

She had been driving to pick up Edwin. She wanted to inform him she would be a tad late by sending him a text. First she had hit the send button. Then a tree.

She had to survive this. She had to fight.

But for what?

So that she could go back to being Mrs. Lian. She felt the fight going out of her.

Mrs. Lian was too busy to die. Yet she did.

Blue

Zara walked amongst the rubble as fast as her tiny feet could carry her. The harsh afternoon sun was beating down upon her. She was grateful her mother had cut her hair short. Zara had insisted on going out today and despite what her better judgment beseeched her to do she let her child go out. It was a ten-minute walk from their home. She wouldn't deny the child such simple pleasures when in all fairness she didn't know if their own house could be termed safe anymore. All she could do was pray for Zara's safety.

A soldier was standing at a distance with a rifle swung over his shoulder. Girls weren't allowed to step out without a male member of the family accompanying them. He glanced in Zara's direction and lost interest presuming her to be a boy. Zara quickened her footsteps. She wanted to reach her happy place faster. The one place that made her forget the chaos that she had grown up with.

She entered the basement which had been converted into a library. Her aunt was seated in a corner and graced her with a faint smile. If the soldiers got the slightest inkling it would be dealt the same fate as all the other buildings in Aleppo. It would be razed to the ground. Zara took out a book from the folds of her dress and placed it on the shelf before picking up another book she had her eyes set on for weeks. That's when she heard it. The ear-splitting crash that had become a routine fixture in her life. She knew the drill. Her aunt was screaming at her to get down on the floor. But she didn't go through the motions like the always did. The direction from which the sound emanated made her climb up a chair to peek out through the sole window in the basement. A queer coldness had begun to tighten its grip around the nine year old's heart. Her eyes fervently tried to locate the blue curtains that framed the window on the third floor of the building next the leafless tree. Her home.

Zara stood by the dusty window, clutching a book to her chest with tears blurring her vision as she saw the faded sky-blue curtains flutter in the air momentarily before landing on the debris below which she had called home minutes before.

Dreamcatchers

One minute he was sitting in the living room playing The Dreamcatchers video game. The next minute he was running through a dense forest trying to evade the fire-breathing monster chasing him. He was trapped inside the game with no way out. His lungs felt like they were on fire. The monster closed in on him and he let out a blood curling cry as all hope had been lost.

The nurses at the asylum sighed. Their hearts heavy with pity for the boy screaming and running circles in his rooms.

Treasure

In the murky depths of the ocean, the divers found the remnants of the Desaru shipwreck. A school of fish darted away at alarming speed at the approach of the divers. Amidst the rotting wood and unruly sea weed, they found the skeleton of the pirate clutching his most valuable piece of treasure. She too was a skeleton.

Muffled Voices

Every year on her birthday he would bring her purple orchids. Her favourite flower. He didn't break tradition on that hot summer afternoon as he placed the orchids on her grave. A tear ran down his cheek.

"I miss you, Anna." he said, his voice choked with tears.

"And I miss you," she said. But he had already walked away.

She sighed.

No one could hear her from six feet under. The earth seemed to muffle her voice.

Memories

Every morning for the past decade he would wake up and plant a kiss on her cheek. Her hazel eyes sparkled with the faintest specks of gold as she smiled back at him. He had loved her for years and he would continue to love her for years to come. Nothing had changed.

His wife calls out to him for breakfast and he closes the wallet containing the photograph of the woman he had loved and lost.

Proud

Squirming my way into jeans, sucking in my belly while wearing a tightly knit blouse, saying no to that cheesecake slice at dinner was an everyday routine during high school. It didn't help that added to my weight troubles, I was also far from what someone would call fair skinned.

I belonged to a country where thin, long-legged, blemish free Bollywood actresses are worshipped. Companies sell fairness creams like hotcakes and every second advertisement urges you to consume some god awful concoction to lose weight.

As a sixteen year old I wanted nothing more than to look like those gorgeous women that grace magazines. And I cleaned up quite nicely. Or so I thought I did.

Lost all the weight. Fit into the skinniest pair of jeans I had my heart set on for eons. Avoided the sun like I was a vampire from a B-grade horror movie. Gulped down numerous cups of green tea for that precious "skin glow" you are promised. In short, I put myself through hell.

On one sunny afternoon in Goa I sat with my legs dangling in the pool with my boyfriend seated next to me. I was still a tad uncomfortable with the sun gazing down on me but I was willing to make an exception on vacation.

"You must have been quite the "chubster" back in your day" he said with a broad grin on his face as he traced a finger along my thigh.

"What?"

"Those stretch marks running from your hips." he answered with a proud look on his face like he had solved an airtight puzzle.

I felt sixteen again. Those old insecurities slowly clawing their way back in.

"I wasn't *that* fat."

"It doesn't matter. You aren't fat now. Would've been nice if you didn't have those stretch marks though." he said nonchalantly before diving into the pool.

I sat there, dumbfounded. All those years of trying to adhere to the description of what society called "beautiful" and yet I wasn't beautiful enough.

And that's when it hit me. You can lose all the weight and slather yourself with fairness creams. You can avoid that delicious burger and drink lemon water instead. Someone will always find a way to show you how flawed you are. You will be too fat. Too thin. Too dark. Too fair. Too tall. Too short.

For the first time I can say I gave up and I am proud that I did. I gave up on those terrifying diets and those pesky so called beauty regimes.

I don't say no to extra cheese anymore.

I wear bikinis even though I have stretch marks.

I go to bed without my face caked with gooey creams.

Luis

Alberto often came to rest by the banks of the river after a busy day. The stillness of the waters and the thick foliage surrounding the banks calmed his nerves and streamlined his thoughts. The bright moon compensated for the dearth of stars in the night sky. Everything around him looked eerily beautiful. Ever since that journalist had written a piece about his village, tourists had come flocking to his hometown in large numbers. He had begun to depend less and less on his dying fishing business and more on being a tour guide. He decided it would be best to cater to the needs of the tourists till their enthusiasm stayed alive and once the tourism trickled down he would return to fishing. Perhaps he could even ask Karla's hand in marriage by the end of summer provided he had saved up a bit. He was immersed in his thoughts when he spotted the slightest of movements near a clump of wild plantain on the far end of the river bank and made his way towards it.

The beast was nearly fifteen feet long. It was the colour of powdered emeralds and ash. A thin layer of silt from the river coated its scales. It's yellow eyes were half closed as if it were in a trance. Alberto cautiously took a step back. Crocodiles were startlingly fast despite their hefty girth. He didn't want to make any sudden movements to alert the green monster and delicately inched backwards when he noticed the spatter of blood above its left eye. Copious amounts of blood was oozing out of a hole the size of a bottle cap above its eye. He'd been fixated on getting away with all his limbs intact earlier he had not noticed the crocodile's injury. He'd often heard stories of farmers shooting crocodiles when their cattle ventured too close to river banks, making themselves easy prey. But this was the first time he had actually seen an injured beast.

Every muscle in his body screamed for him to turn in the opposite direction and leave. He began to walk back home. Pragmatism and logic dictated his moves. But something began to gnaw at him from within. The village was exploding at a terrifying pace. More people. More mouths to feed. More jobs required. More land being brought under cultivation. More.

Everyone trying their best to stay afloat and survive. He didn't see how this yellow eyed beast was any different. The humans had encroached upon its space. It was only natural for it to retaliate by preying on what belonged to them in order to ensure it survived.

He quickened his pace. He found some old bed sheets and two metal poles. He fashioned an odd looking yet sturdy stretcher in no time. He contemplated enlisting Daniel's help but figured it would take a ton of time and effort to convince him to lug such a menacing beast back home.

When he reached the river bank, the valorous thoughts flooding his mind earlier had dissipated into thin air. He had no prior experience with animals much less a scaly injured reptile. Rationality began to take over. It was an injured animal that was undoubtedly feeling vulnerable which meant it would attack if he got too close. Why in the wold would it trust him, a human? He suppressed the thoughts and placed the makeshift stretcher beside it. Tiny beads of sweat had formed on Alberto's forehead.

He gingerly placed the makeshift stretcher as close to the crocodile as possible. Unsure of how to approach it he decided the shift had to be done quickly. Like pulling off a Band-Aid, he said to himself. But the mantra did little to calm his nerves. When he clutched its tail and moved the lower part of its body onto the stretcher he realized how emaciated it really was. It had perhaps been lying on the river banks for days or even weeks judging from its weight. It weighed merely half a quintal he guessed. It didn't put up a fight like he had assumed it would.

Alberto now stood a spitting distance from the snout of the crocodile. One snap of its jaws around his legs and he would be a goner for sure. He cursed himself for impulsive thoughts and firmly placed his palms around its neck. Taking painstaking care not to move its head too much and aggravate the wound, he managed to get the entire crocodile onto the stretcher. He wasn't quite sure if he was impressed with himself for single-handedly moving the crocodile or accomplishing the feat with none of his limbs being chewed off. He grabbed the poles jutting out at the end of the stretcher near the tail and slowly drew the stretcher home. He was grateful for the cloak of abandonment the night had laid on the streets. He would make for an extremely odd sight. For the first time in years, Alberto was grateful his hut was located close to the river, away from the bustling market. Apart from his own hut, there were two or three more similar huts along the path lined with peepal trees. Solitude was a gift indeed.

Months went by as he kept the scaly beast hidden from sight and slowly nursed it back to health. A constant smell of chicken and rice and the swamp enveloped Alberto's house. The crocodile hadn't growled or hissed even once. Except in the initial week when he tried to extract the bullet. Eventually it relented and Alberto had succeeded in retrieving the bullet and dressing the gaping hole as well as his inexperienced hands could. He called him Luis. He made multiple visits to the local vet asking seemingly innocent questions about how to treat gunshot wounds. Every week he would cycle to the neighbouring town to fetch medicines for there were no stores selling the same in his own village. He knew people would call him crazy or worse — harm Luis. He promised himself he would keep it a secret and once Luis had made a full recovery he would take him back to the river. There was always the threat of Luis turning on him once he had surpassed his convalescent stage but Alberto refused to entertain such nefarious thoughts.

Luis had begun to gain most of the weight he had lost. His recovery was nothing short of a miracle. With each passing day he would look more robust and muscular. When Alberto placed banana leaves heaped with a mixture of chicken rice, Luis would nudge him with his snout. At first Alberto was taken aback. He didn't have an inkling about how he was supposed to interpret that gesture. But gradually he learnt it was merely Luis gruff way of expressing his gratitude.

Alberto had completely given up going to the river. He spent every passing minute tending to Luis. He replaced his bandages. Restocked his food and water supplies. When he got home he had gotten into a strange habit of calling out to Luis. What was even more peculiar was Luis responding by slowly dragging himself towards Alberto to acknowledge his return. The duo had settled into a comfortable routine. They weren't two animals of different species. They were friends.

Summer went by and it seemed to Karla that she wouldn't be walking down the aisle anytime soon. She had begun to grow suspicious. It had been months since she laid eyes on Alberto and when she did get a minute of his time he would blame the tourists. The workload was getting out of hand he would say offhandedly and scurry away. He'd even stopped inviting her to his place. It had been a tradition of sorts for the two of them to cook together every fortnight and laze by the river bank. It was the one luxury they allowed themselves in a time when money was running precariously low as Alberto was saving every penny to build them a proper house to move into once they got married. They had a plan. They had envisioned their future together. But now something had changed. She could see it in Alberto's eyes. He seemed worried about something else. Or someone else she thought.

One evening, she mustered up the courage to confront Alberto. It would be better to get her heart broken now than to get into a loveless marriage like that of her parents. She saw the pain in Alberto's eyes when she asked him what was truly going on. She braced herself for the inevitable. But he beseeched her to come home to dispel her fears.

Alberto wasn't entirely confident how Karla would react but this was his best shot at not losing the woman he so dearly loved. She was a woman made of grit and strength. She didn't go screaming with arms flailing in the opposite direction. When her eyes fell on Luis a faint gasp escaped her lips but she stood her ground. A string of words escaped from Alberto. He narrated the entire episode without a pause hoping he was framing his sentences coherently. Without a word she walked away.

The next morning, she asked him who was paying for the medicines, for the meals of that horrendous beast which would devour him whole any second it feels strong enough to get back up on its feet on its own. She spat out vitriolic words upon learning it was his savings, which had depleted close to nothing, that had funded the animal's upkeep. It took Alberto every ounce of energy to convince her to stay. Luis would be returned to the wild, he promised. A few more days and Luis can venture out into the river alone. Karla wasn't elated but she was willing to meet him half way. She responded with a curt nod.

A few days later, Alberto called out to Luis. The sun was setting in the horizon, throwing shades of salmon and orange all around. Luis trailed behind Alberto. When they reached the river bank, Alberto sensed Luis' hesitation. Alberto made the first move. He walked into the river till the water reached his waist and called out to Luis. After a few more seconds of apprehension, Luis eased his scaly body into the river. The dying sunlight glanced off his majestic body. Luis swam towards Alberto and flipped upside down. To a bystander, the spectacle would send a cold shiver down their spine. But Alberto was used to Luis and his mannerisms. He knew he wasn't in any danger. Luis just wanted to play. This was the least he could do before he bade Luis goodbye. He stayed in the water till the sun had disappeared and the moon had unleashed her silver reign on the sky. A gnawing had begun within Alberto's belly once more. But this was different from the time he had first met Luis. He didn't want to say goodbye. He placed a soft kiss on Luis snout. His mind went back to all those months ago when he was downright terrified of touching Luis, let alone plant a kiss on that snout concealing gigantic teeth. He slowly waded out of the water and made his way home. When he looked back, there was no sign of Luis. The unblemished surface of the river reflected the ivory moon with not even a ripple in sight.

The next morning, Alberto went through his usual routine forgetting last night's farewell. He plucked a few banana leaves from the stack of leaves next to the stove and began stirring some rice and chicken in a pot when it struck him. Luis was gone. It would take a while to get used to the emptiness prevailing in his home. The comfortable routine was now broken. He emptied the contents of the pot into the wastebasket and decided to sit on the back-porch of the hut before jetting off to work. But the door was jammed. It wouldn't budge. He walked out through the front door and made it to his porch only to find the cause of the jammed door. Luis was sprawled on the back porch. All fifteen feet of his humongous body was resting against the hut's wall. His friend had come back. Luis was finally home.

Rita's Hope

A thick fog draped the streets of Mumbai that cold morning.

She stood outside the gates. Peering in, knowing full well she wouldn't get a glimpse but she couldn't sit around and do nothing. Rita's family was not going to let her in. Mrs. Kumar had hurled every form of insult and accusation she could think of.

"I lost my daughter because of you," she had screamed at her before the other relatives had beseeched her to leave.

"You ruined her life, do you want to ruin her funeral as well?" her mother managed to spit out between sobs.

Yesterday they had been holding hands and walking along Marine drive. Today Rita lay on the other side of those wrought iron gates surrounded by people who hadn't understood her, her whole life. Those very people were the reason for Rita being gone today, she thought.

She didn't feel an iota of grief. It was unsettling. She just felt numb. She kept repeating, "Rita is gone" in her head like a mantra. Trying to make it sound real. Trying to believe.

That's when she saw the pall bearers carrying a bundle wrapped in white. She caught a glimpse of her face. The numbness began to melt away. The fact that Rita was gone finally registered. She ran all the way home, tears stinging her eyes.

She lived in a country run by murderous politicians, bribery was rampant, rape was a common occurrence, dowry was expected rather than shunned and child marriage was acceptable.

Yet Section 377 loomed over those like Rita and her. The bitter truth was that love was a crime in her incredible country.

She had always been the pessimist. Every rally they attended, every article they wrote, every act of defiance had seemed pointless to her.

"They won't change, Rita. Not in a million years." she would say.

It was Rita who believed she could change the world. And now she lay dead in a house filled with hypocrites.

The strongest woman I know killed herself. What chance do I possibly have to survive this? To make a difference, she thought.

Rita's pale face kept swirling in her mind. She could end it all just like Rita had and put herself out of this misery. But for what? What purpose did that serve?

She had to live. She had to fight. She had to keep Rita's hope alive. And maybe someday, just maybe love would no longer be a crime.

Hazel Eyes

She stood under the awning of the book shop waiting for him. Sean paced up and down the sidewalk, his brows furrowed as he rapidly spoke into the phone. She knew the conversation wouldn't end soon. Work calls never do. But she didn't blame him. If her phone rang, with Rosie from marketing on the other end, she'd be pacing up and down trying to sort out the office shenanigans too. Thoughts of how the two of them got stuck in the rat race, how they became such massive corporate sell-outs kept swirling in her mind when she saw *him* in the store adjacent to the bookshop.

He had soft hazel eyes and chocolate brown hair that appeared to be flecked with gold when the sunlight grazed it in the right angle. Something about him just screamed happy. She hadn't seen someone *that* genuinely delighted on a mundane Sunday afternoon. Her heart curiously skipped a beat. She momentarily forgot Sean and walked into the store. He caught sight of her too and it just clicked. He wouldn't stop wagging his tail as she approached the tiny basket he was placed in.

Sean placed his cell phone in his coat pocket and searched the pavement for Anna. She was walking out of the pet store with a fur-ball in one hand who was squirming to lick her face, while she carried a huge bag undoubtedly filled with supplies to care for the little one in the other hand.

"I leave you alone for a minute and this happens," Sean muttered waving his hand in the general direction of the puppy.

Before she could say anything, he was trying to get out of Anna's arms in order to reach for Sean.

"Goddammit," Sean sighed with a smile threatening to break out on his face before he took the tiny one into his arms.

The Steak

"Nancy, the girl at table five wants to have a word with you," said Linda apprehensively. Nancy was just getting ready to head out. Linda knew there couldn't have been a worse time.

"Ask Frank to deal with it."

"He did. But the girl insists on talking to the head-chef."

Two girls who appeared to be in their early twenties were seated at table five. The brunette with the curly hair, perfectly drawn winged eyeliner and a garish red pout shot a vitriolic glance towards Nancy.

"I was told you wish to speak to me." said Nancy.

"This steak is a joke," the brunette said.

The other girl wearing oversized glasses sans lenses was viciously concentrating on the glowing screen before her, her fingers typing away with alarming speed, completely oblivious to the altercation which was undoubtedly going to go down.

"Excuse me?" Nancy was not used to being addressed with such insolence.

"You heard me. This steak is garbage. Nothing about it is right."

"Pray tell what is wrong with it."

"The colour of the steak doesn't look right when I apply the filter."

"Filter?"

The brunette rolled her eyes as far back into her head as she could before replying, "Instagram. Filters. Pictures. Does that ring a bell?"

Nancy now noticed the girl's plate. It was untouched. Not even a bite. The sauce had begun to congeal. God knows how long this imbecile had kept the steak untouched, acting like she is a wildlife photographer whose next paycheck depended on this one perfect shot, thought Nancy.

"I tried every angle. And don't even get me started about the lighting in this place," continued the brunette.

"And the network," murmured the bespectacled girl as she left the table frantically waving her phone in the air trying to get a signal.

"What is it with you kids these days? Do you have to document every meal you eat?" Nancy asked, her ill temper threatening to rear its ugly head. Nancy could hear Linda clearing her throat in the background.

"I like taking pictures of my food, Grandma," came the tart reply which was sufficient to throw Nancy over the edge.

Nancy snapped her fingers behind her back and another steak appeared on the table. The brunette was nowhere to be seen.

"So do I," Nancy said with an amused chuckle before clicking a picture with her ancient phone that had an awful camera. She turned her back on the table and began making her way to the kitchen when she saw Linda rushing towards her. Her face a sickly shade of purple. Before Nancy could reach the kitchen door, Linda grabbed her shoulder.

"Are you crazy? Is this how you get your kicks, Nancy? Just gulp down a few drinks like a normal person instead. Someone could have seen you."

"It's almost closing time. No one is around."

"Turn her back!"

"I will but not yet. Let her marinate in the sauces for a while. That ought to teach her a…"

Before Nancy could complete her sentence, Linda's nails were digging into Nancy's shoulder, her eyes had grown wider than usual. Nancy followed Linda's gaze to find the bespectacled girl back at the table picking up a fork and a knife. She was reaching out to the fresh steak on the table.

Nancy snapped her fingers rushing towards the table. A tiny sliver of meat was already pierced between the tines of the fork. The brunette appeared out of nowhere covered with a thin film of sauce and a sprinkling of herbs.

The two girls looked washed out. Nancy was scanning the girl from head to toe making sure her fried hadn't mangled her in any way. The girl seemed fine with all her limbs intact. Only a large chunk of her curly hair was missing above her left ear.

The slightest of whimpers escaped their lips as they fled the restaurant with all the speed they could muster up. They had left their phones behind.

There was no trace of the girls when Linda had finally steadied her wobbly limbs and walked over to Nancy.

"Customer is king or some gibberish to that effect. Ever heard of that?" Linda said through gritted teeth.

The Winged Curse

"Can you believe the number of gullible people out there? They actually believe in *this*," Richard said prodding the papier-mâché figurine lying on his desk

Darren shifted uncomfortably but did not voice his opinion.

"God. Don't tell me you believe in it too? Sarah made it. It's not real."

"Well, then she should have posted it on the Internet herself. It's her handiwork after all. Why give it to us?"

"She is a prop maker, you blubbering nut. People would have seen right through it. It's just an April Fool's prank. We'll pull the plug on it once the hullabaloo dies down. No harm done."

Richard gingerly picked the "dead fairy" off his desk and examined it. One could see the blackish-grey rotting skin stretch over the rib cage and the almost ash like wings protruding from either side of the spinal cord. If he didn't know any better he would've agreed with Darren.

"Sarah sure does have a knack for detail," Darren chimed in as he slipped into his coat and left.

Richard checked his pager and cellphone one last time out of habit before going to bed. The minute his head hit the pillow sleep had overtaken him. A few hours later he felt a heavy weight pressing on his chest. His eyes slowly fluttered open. It took a few seconds for his groggy eyes to adjust to the darkness.

And that's when he saw it. A rotting faceless creature with wings spanning five feet sitting on top of him. It was the exact replica of the figurine except it was magnified a million times. A scream was bubbling in his throat when it clutched his neck. Its nails were digging into his flesh.

"It's always the same charade with you humans. The screaming. The crying. At least Sarah had the courtesy to faint when I approached her. A much quieter option," the creature whispered into his ears. He could feel it's sour breath against his skin.

"I won't hurt you. Not much at least. All I ask in return is a favour," it continued in a tone that sounded like a mix between a hiss and a whisper. "It started in Cottingley. And it soon spread. Keeping fairies as *pets*. They kept us locked and chained, plucked our wings out for merriment. Thousands of us died because of the vile human offsprings. But I was one of the few to survive. Black magic coupled with blood lust can make you quite powerful, I have learnt. Yet, I need you to be my vessel. Your workplace suits me quite nicely. I can't enter a place without being summoned or carried in. I have found that hovering around in open spaces to prey on children is quite laborious since their miserable parents are always around. So I can I count on you, Richard? To be my vessel?" it said and let out a half snicker, half wail.

Tiny droplets of blood ran down Richard's neck as the creature's grip tightened with every passing second. Richard nodded faintly.

Doctor Richard Pearson walked into the paediatric ward the next morning with a "dead fairy" in his pocket.

The Withering of Coral Jasmines

Centuries ago a mortal princess named Parijata fell in love with the Sun God – Surya. But as it goes with all forms of fledgling love, it begins to fray and gradually fades into oblivion. The bonds of love between Surya and Parijata were no exception. It dawned upon Surya that he wouldn't be able to shun his duties any longer else mortals would suffer. Flash floods, hailstorms and torrential downpour had already begun to wash away homes. Inundated fields and drowning animals became a common sighting. Varuna had unleashed his reign. Surya had to return to his throne in the heavens above if he hoped to reverse even a sliver of the havoc his own flesh and blood had wreaked.

Parijata had led all her life within the walls of the Royal Palace without an inkling of the merciless realities that prevailed out in the real world. Surya's abandonment was the first loss she had ever been subjected to. He'd left behind an empty shell of a woman who found living with sorrow clawing at the walls of her heart too great a burden.

The very next day after the princess' cremation, the morose king visited his daughter's grave only to find a spectacular tree growing atop her grave which seemed to have sprung up overnight. It was the Tree of Sorrow.

When the waxen moon is suspended amongst the shimmering stars in the black satin sky, the coral jasmine blooms on the branches of the Tree of Sorrow. She unfurls her gossamer like white petals to reveal a vibrant coral centre which emanates the most intoxicating fragrance. These button-sized flowers cover the entire tree making it difficult to discern the jade foliage underneath. But as the first soft rays of the sun trickle through the ashen sky hundreds of coral jasmines fall to the ground and wither away. The tree is sans flowers at day break with her magnificence visible only under the quietude of the night The blossoms choose to shrivel into brown translucent shreds and become one with the earth rather than have the liquid gold light of the sun rays taint their white petals as his superficial love had once tainted the princess's heart.

Escaping the Limbo

A peculiar numbness enveloped her.
A gash, a cut and she would feel
Something, anything albeit only momentarily.
A cowardly act, she was well aware.
As the saying goes,
cut sideways for attention
cut lengthwise for results.
She wasn't sure when
she would switch to the latter.
She was stuck in a limbo.
Too tired to live. Too afraid to die.

SS Mohegan

I was making my way out of one of the hatchway's of the SS Mohegan into the emerald expanse when I saw Thomas. He was frantically signalling to me from a distance. Thomas despised the sea. I had warned him not to wander off to far. "Thalassophobia," he would say in an attempt to sound smarter than the rest of us. But he was trying those corny "overcome your fears" resolutions and I had suggested wreck diving. I began to swim towards him hoping he wasn't chickening out already. I was hell bent on not going back up without a souvenir or two to sell online.

The murky water had made it difficult to discern the figure who had been signalling earlier. A sickly pale man with rotting greenish grey flesh was floating towards me. Flesh had peeled off in chunks to reveal the bones underneath. Thomas was nowhere to be seen. They say panic is your worst enemy underwater. I was starting to understand why. I tried to squirm away from that hideous thing when I felt its bony hand grip my wrist.

"We must save her. I can't let her go down. I won't abandon her. I owe it to her. I owe it to my crew," it said in a hoarse voice as it dragged me deeper into the caverns of the rust coated wreck.

A flutter of relief exploded in my heart when I spotted two other divers a mere seven feet away from us. The distance dwindled away until I was right beside them and yet they didn't even grace me with a glance. And that's when I saw it. Their bloated bodies floated in the water. One of them wore a wet suit with my initials on it. The other had my brother's initials. The one Thomas had borrowed.

A queer numbness began to assault my senses. I could feel the darkness closing in upon me.

I was making my way out of one of the hatchways of the SS Mohegan into the emerald expanse when I saw Thomas. He was frantically signalling to me from a distance.

A Mother's Sorrow

The leaves twirled in a melancholic haze
as they fell to the snow laden ground.
The last granule of sand had slipped
into the bottom bulb of the hourglass
The cold crept its way
deep into Demeter's heart.
It was time for Persephone
to return to the underworld.
The snow sparkled like shards of diamonds
whilst the glimmer in Demeter's eyes faded.
Winter was nothing more than
the manifestation of a mother's sorrow.

Tradition

You don't need that slice of cake, Mama said.
Classmates snickered at the 'whale in a dress'
Her first kiss was
the by-product of pity churning in his heart
Inner beauty?
There's no such thing, the world screamed.
She wanted to change
and change she did.
But the blessed tradition of body shaming
She kept alive
When she called her baby girl fat.

Destroy

The moonlight lent a touch of silver to the dark rustling forest. She stepped out of her home and walked towards the nearby woods. Streaks of moonlight filtered through the canopy of leaves. She walked upon the soft bed of moss and pine needles. The air was laced with the scent of moon flowers. She could hear the musical whispers again. Ever since she had moved into her new home, she often heard these soft voices. Tonight she'd followed them. She had to find out what they were telling her. They sounded so devastatingly beautiful. In a hypnotic gaze she followed the voices.

She reached a clearing in the midst of the foliage. Hundreds of winged beauties hovered in a circle. They fluttered their translucent purple-veined wings in unison and she could finally discern the message the voices had chanted since the day she moved into her new home.

"You belong here with us," they chorused.

She felt like she had finally come home. A sense of belonging enveloped her. With the moon showing them the path, they led her deeper into the forest. She stood at the edge of a cliff. The waves crashed against the jagged rocks below. She could taste the sea salt on her lips. The tiny winged creatures continued to whisper.

"Jump" they said.

So she did.

The faeries of the forest felt satiated. The forest sighed a content sigh.

The house on the edge of the woods had annihilated the home of the faeries. They could not forget the chaos as the saws slashed their dwellings built in the crevices of the majestic trees. The vile family had to pay. The faeries had collected their debt under gaze of the ashen moon.

A thin figure lay on the rocks below as the waves lapped upon her contorted body.

Melancholia

Her voice was like the sea caressing the shore,
Like a gentle breeze whistling through the woods.
It calmed his nerves at times like these.
He sat in the study soaked in the dying light of the day
Drumming his fingers ever so lightly
As her song transported him to the old days.
If only he had sensed the melancholia
Entwined in the beauty of her lyrics
Perhaps he could have saved her from herself.
If only he had read between the lines of her songs
She would be by his side singing her tune.
But her music was a vessel that held her grief
And when it was filled to the brim
She had to say goodbye.
But the memory of her would forever remain
In the tunes she played for him.

Stillness

The pink mound of flesh she held was moving and stretching its arms. Its piercing blue eyes looked at her as it yearned to touch her pale face. The odour of spit and vomit emanated from it. Her nipples felt raw from feeding it. The stitches sent a shooting pain up her abdomen every time she moved. She slouched next to the bathtub unable to move. The cold bathroom tiles pressing against her legs soothed her. The sound of the water gushing into the ceramic tub lulled her senses. If only she could put it down for a minute and shut her eyes. It began wailing the very second she loosened her grip. It began clawing at her sweater wanting to be fed again. She gently lowered it into the lukewarm water in the tub. The warmth seemed to comfort the squealing creature.

She let go.

A few bubbles dotted the surface of the water before stillness was restored. She stretched herself out on the cold floor and slept like a baby.

A Glimmer of Light

She wears ink on her skin
And a short blue dress
She dances the night away
With a drink in her hand.

She stumbles a bit
And leans on her friend
The hazy lights in the hallway
Make her head spin.

Fatigue takes over
And all she wants is to go home
But promises of being taken care of
Are whispered in her ear.

As she waits in the car
Not a sliver of worry clouds her mind
For she is with a friend.
A trusted friend.

He thought he broke her soul that night
The world said :
"Provocative clothes and too many drinks
Something was bound to go wrong"

He showed no remorse.
Yet, no one asked the pertinent question,
"Why has consent become a thing of the past?
In which other atrocity is the victim blamed?"

But she was a fighter.
A raging survivor.
A glimmer of light she would find in the storm.
Not him, not the world could ever take her down.

The Broken Bride

One minute the air was thick with the scent of jasmines,
The next, plumes of smoke and sharp cries filled the air.

A shooting pain stirred her awake.
Her wedding had ended and the nightmare had begun.

Her hands previously adorned with red henna
Were now dark red with blood.

The airstrike had claimed her family, her love
Yet, a stroke of twisted luck had spared her life.

She wasn't given the luxury of holding a funeral
For the bodies were never recovered.

The country never acknowledged the attack.
The world carried on as if nothing had ever happened.

She had her own demons to battle.
She fled her war-torn homeland.

With a fervent hope of rebuilding her life,
She set out to find refuge, a place she could call home.

Only to be turned down
By the very same country that had shattered her life.

Also By Chapeltown Books

Spectrum
by Christopher Bowles

A collection of one hundred and ten pieces of flash-fiction and poetry. You probably won't like all of them, and some of them might even disgust you, or make you uncomfortable. But stick with it. Look at overarching themes within each coloured block. Find the puns in certain titles. Research the colours that you've never heard of. Try and work out which stories are complete fabrications, which ones contain nuggets of truth, and which ones are versions of real life events.

Order from Amazon:

ISBN: 978-1-910542-13-2 (paperback)
978-1-910542-14-9 (ebook)

Chapeltown Books

Fog Lane
by Neil Campbell

Fog Lane is a collection of stories about memory. Many of the stories have been published online and in magazines. They were written over a long period of time. The oldest, *The Rose Garden* was first written in about 2007 and published in Orbis. The last one in the book, *Here Comes the Sun,* was completed in 2017. The stories in this book vary from the humorous to the sad to the macabre. They are all short stories of under a thousand words.

Order from Amazon:

ISBN: 978-1-910542-08-8 (paperback)
978-1-910542-09-5 (ebook)

Chapeltown Books

January Stones
by Gill James

These stories were written one a day throughout January 2013. They were originally published on a blog called Gill's January Stones. Sometimes the stories would come right at the beginning of the day. Sometimes they would take a while longer.

Do they have a theme? Not really, though the idea of 'stones' is one of turning them over slowly on the beach until we find the right one.

There was no strict word count. Each story is as long as it needs to be. It had to be finished, though, by midnight of that day.

Order from Amazon:

ISBN: 978-1-910542-10-1 (paperback)
978-1-910542-11-8 (ebook)

Chapeltown Books